First published in the United States, Great Britain, Canada, Australia, and New Zealand in 2014
by NorthSouth Books Inc., an imprint of NordSüd Verlag AG, CH-8005, Zürich, Switzerland.

Distributed in the United States by NorthSouth Books Inc., New York 10016.
Library of Congress Cataloging-in-Publication Data is available.
Printed in China by Hung Hing Co., Ltd., Guangdong, July 2014.
ISBN: 978-0-7358-4177-2
1 3 5 7 9 • 10 8 6 4 2

www.northsouth.com

Stefanie Dahle

Lily,
the Little Elf Princess

A picture storybook

North
South

The sun had just risen above Water Lily Castle, but Lily, the little elf princess, had been awake for a long time. She was making garlands of wildflowers and singing an old elfin song. Her animal friends gathered beside her.

"Finished at last!" Lily cried, putting
a garland on the head of Trotty, the little forest snuffle.
Then she gave him a big kiss on the nose.

"You sing beautifully," said Trotty, blushing.

"Singing? What use is that?" mumbled Minnie, the meadow snipe.

Lily laughed. "Would you like a garland too?"

"I suppose it couldn't hurt," moaned Minnie.

Then Lily said, "I'm going to bake a honey cake. But first I have
to visit the little hedgehog fairy and the other animals."

"Who are you going to bake the cake for?" asked Trotty, climbing onto a root stool.

"Today's the day of the Elf Party!" said Lily, tending to the wound on the fat dormouse. "I promised to take garlands and honey cake."

"There's no water-lily honey today," hummed the honeylings, who just then came buzzing through the window of Water Lily Castle.

"We couldn't collect any because all the water lilies on Lake Magic have closed their petals."

"No honey for my honey cake? But I need to bake one!" cried the elf princess.

She was very upset, and hurried to Lake Magic to have a look at the water lilies.

It was true! All the water lilies
in the lake had closed their petals.
Hard as she tried, Lily simply could
not think why.

Suddenly the elf princess heard
a quiet sobbing. Among the leaves
of the water lilies she saw her friend,
the little nymph Freya, with tears
streaming down her face.

"Hello, Freya," said Lily gently.
"Why are you so sad?"

"Oh, Lily," sobbed the nymph.
"I don't want to sit forever with all
these frogs in the water. I'd so love
to go dancing! And this evening is the
great Elf Party."

"Then why don't you simply come
to the party?" asked Lily, in surprise.

"I can't," said Freya unhappily. "A
nymph can only leave her pool when
the water lilies open their petals."

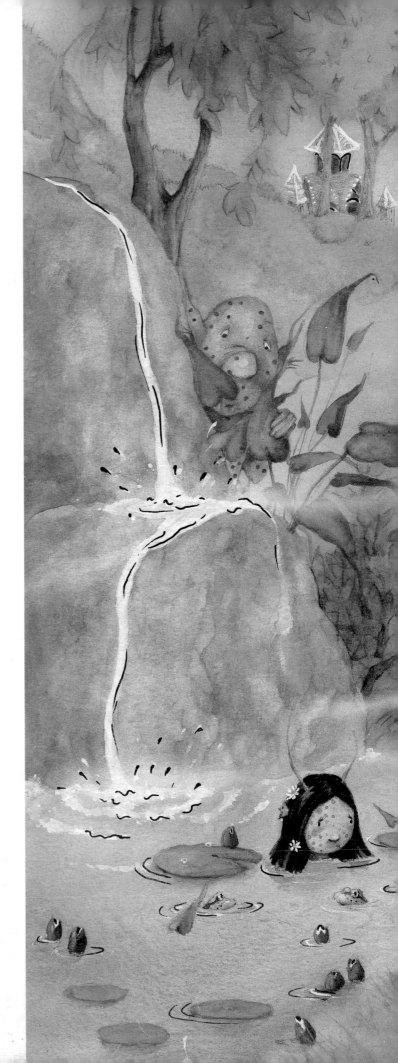

"But why have the water lilies closed their petals?" asked Lily. "I thought all flowers opened at sunrise."

Freya shook her head. "Not water lilies. They wake up only when I play my flute under the willow."

The little nymph pointed toward an old willow tree, whose branches hung far out over the water as the tree creakily nodded its head.

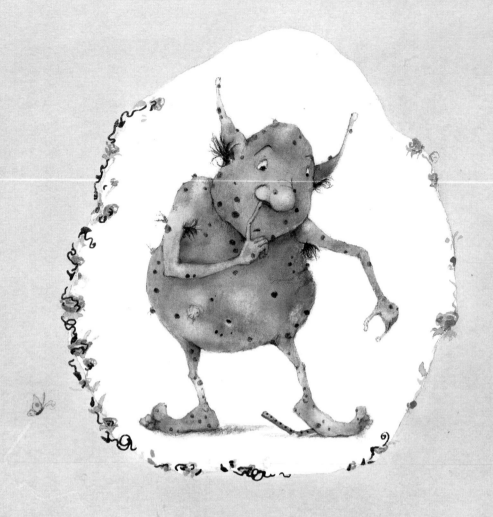

"The water-lily petals have been closed since yesterday—a big fat forest troll stepped on my flute and broke it! Perhaps you can help me?" Freya held the broken flute out to Lily.

"I'm sorry," said Lily when she saw the flute. "I can't mend it. But I'm sure I can find someone who can open the water lilies."

Lily gently lifted one of the plants out of the water together with its roots. "Don't be sad," she said to Freya. "I'll think of something, I promise."

Then the little elf princess set out with Trotty the forest snuffle and Minnie the snipe. Who could help Freya? she wondered. Maybe the big elves?

Lily and her friends climbed into her swan boat
and headed toward Elf Town, where there was
sure to be someone who would know what to do.

The Light Elf lived on the very edge of the village. "Hello, Lily," she said, welcoming the little elf princess. "I see you've brought a water lily with you. Are you going to plant it in your lake?"

"No," said Lily. "I want the water lilies to open so that Freya can leave Lake Magic. Can you help me?"

The Light Elf quickly reached for a small bottle of sparkling liquid. "This is light," she explained, sprinkling some over the water lily. "Light is like a magic spell that makes flowers blossom."

But nothing happened. The water lily remained tightly closed.

"That's too bad," said Trotty, trying to comfort Lily. "But I'm sure you'll soon find someone else who can open it."

In a clearing Lily met the
Meadow Elf with his unicorn.

"Hello, Lily!" cried the Meadow
Elf. "Shall we go for a ride together?"

"I'm afraid I don't have time," said Lily.
"I'm looking for someone to show me how to make
water lilies open their petals."

She held up the water lily, and the Meadow Elf
thought for a moment. Then he whispered something in
the ear of his unicorn. Through his nostrils, the unicorn blew
glittering stardust over the water lily.

Lily couldn't help giggling. The stardust tickled her nose.

"What a lot of nonsense!" murmured Minnie, with a loud cough.

But the unicorn's stardust didn't help either. The water lily was still tightly closed.

"Unicorn stardust usually solves any problem,"
said the Meadow Elf. "I'm sorry, Lily."

"I'll just have to try again," Lily said to herself. "The Forest Elf simply has to know what needs to be done. Forest elves know all there is to know about plants."

The Forest Elf waved to her from the trees. "Hello, Lily. Do you need a few dragonflies for your garden? I hope not, because the dragonflies aren't flying today. They say it's too much of a drag!"

"No, I just want to open this water lily, but no one can help me," said the little elf princess.

"Well now, let's have a look," said the Forest Elf. "Maybe it needs to be planted." He picked up a flowerpot and put the water lily in it. Then he covered the roots with some damp earth.

Nothing happened. The water lily remained closed.

"It was obvious that wouldn't help!" groaned Minnie.

"Oh dear," sighed Lily. She so wanted to help Freya. But what could she do? In despair, she set out for Water Lily Castle.

When the elf princess arrived back at Lake Magic, the sun had almost set. In the distance Lily could see a glow. It came from the lanterns of the elves who were climbing up Elf Mountain.

"The party's about to begin," she whispered. "Oh, Freya is going to be so sad that she can't go. And without her, the Elf Party won't be any fun for me, either."

Lily sat down in the grass under the
old willow tree. She looked at the flower in her hand.
The lily was still tightly closed. It was hopeless. Softly
the little elf princess began to hum a sad old elfin melody.
    Sitting beside her, Trotty found the song enchanting. He
closed his eyes, and rocked to and fro with the rhythm.
    And then suddenly something wonderful happened.

The forest animals came out from behind
the trees and bushes, pricking up their ears
at the sound of Lily's voice. Freya too was
drawn to the shore of Lake Magic and listened
spellbound to the song of the elf princess.

The water lily in Lily's hands
began to glitter and glow. Very
slowly, it opened its petals. In
amazement, Lily and Freya
watched as one after another the
water lilies in Lake Magic opened up.

At last the magic spell was broken, and Freya was able to climb out of the water.

"How did you do that? Thank you, Lily!" she cried. Her eyes shone as brightly as the water of the lake.

The little elf looked at the lily in her hands. "I just did what I do best," she said. "I sang."

A tear of joy trickled down Minnie's cheek. "Um, I have something in my eye," she mumbled when Trotty looked at her.

Now the honeylings came buzzing to the lake.
"Look at that!" they hummed. "Look what Lily
did!" Nimbly the honeylings darted from flower
to flower, collecting water-lily honey.

Now it was time for Lily and Freya to
get moving! With elfin speed they baked
a sweet-smelling honey cake, and off
they went to the Elf Party.

Elf Mountain was covered
with festive decorations, and lots of
elves had already arrived—the Light
Elf, the Forest Elf, the Meadow Elf
with his unicorn . . . and the Queen of the
Elves was there too! Everybody was there!

All night, Lily and the little nymph danced the most wonderful dances.
This was the best Elf Party ever!

Even Minnie, the meadow snipe, was leaping around with Trotty.

When dawn began to break, the elf princess embraced her friend Freya.
"Is there anything more beautiful than a party?" she asked with a radiant smile.

"Yes," whispered the happy little nymph. "The most beautiful thing in the
world is a song."